HERE COMES THE PARADE!

written by Tony and Lauren Dungy
with Nathan Whitaker

illustrated by
Vanessa Brantley Newton

Ready-to-Read

Simon Spotlight
New York London Toronto Sydney New Delhi

SIMON SPOTLIGHT
An imprint of Simon & Schuster Children's Publishing Division
1230 Avenue of the Americas, New York, New York 10020
Text copyright © 2014 by Tony Dungy and Lauren Dungy
Illustrations copyright © 2014 by Vanessa Brantley Newton
Published in association with the literary agency of Legacy, LLC, Winter Park, FL 32789
For information about special discounts for bulk purchases, please contact Simon & Schuster Special
Sales at 1-866-506-1949 or business@simonandschuster.com.
Manufactured in the United States of America 0814 LAK
10 9 8 7 6 5 4 3 2
Library of Congress Cataloging-in-Publication Data
Dungy, Tony, author.
Here comes the parade! / by Tony and Lauren Dungy ; illustrated by Vanessa Brantley Newton. — First
edition. pages cm — (Ready-to-read. Level 2)
Summary: When they find a lost wallet at the parade, the Dungy children learn an important lesson about
telling the truth and doing the right thing.
[1. Parades—Fiction. 2. Lost and found possessions—Fiction. 3. Family life—Fiction. 4. Honesty—Fiction.
5. Conduct of life—Fiction.] I. Dungy, Lauren, author. II. Newton, Vanessa, illustrator. III. Title.
PZ7.D9187He 2014 [E]—dc23
2013044795
ISBN 978-1-4424-5469-9 (pbk)
ISBN 978-1-4424-5470-5 (hc)
ISBN 978-1-4424-5471-2 (eBook)

Jade, Jordan, and Justin finally found
just the right spot on the curb
to watch the parade.
Mom and Dad watched
from a few rows back.
They held Jalen and Jason
so they could see too.

WHAT A PARADE!

"I love parades!" shouted Justin.
Jordan and Jade were jumping
up and down,
trying to see over the crowd.

"I can't wait to see the clowns, Jade!"
Jordan yelled.
"I know! Everybody loves clowns,"
Jade answered.
Justin looked nervous.

"I don't think I like clowns,"
Justin said.
"Sure you do," said Jordan.
"They're funny!"
Justin still looked worried.

Jade cheered
as a team of beautiful horses
trotted by.

LOOK WHAT I FOUND!

Next came the shiny red fire trucks.
Behind the trucks,
the kids could see the big floats.
They were getting closer and
closer.

Justin wasn't looking at
the fire trucks.
He was thinking about the clowns
and stared down at the curb.
Then he saw something
on the ground.

"Jordan, Jade, look!"
Justin held up a wallet.
It was very thick.
"That's the funniest looking wallet
I've ever seen," Jade said.

Jordan looked in the wallet
and then looked at Jade.
"There's a ton of money in it,"
he said.

BIG DREAMS

"Can we keep it?" asked Justin.

"I don't know, Justin," Jordan said.

"I sure would like a new football,"
said Justin, "and a new
Ducks shirt, too."

"And I would like a new bracelet," said Jade.
"There's enough to get some fancy, sparkly nail polish, too."

Jordan nodded.
He was thinking about
a fun new phone
and maybe some new games.

Jordan looked at Jade and Justin and asked, "What should we do? You know somebody is looking for their lost wallet."

"We should keep it.
We found it," said Justin.
"I think we should try and find
the owner," said Jordan.

Jade thought for a second and said,
"Maybe we should ask Mom and Dad."

Just then a marching band came by playing a song.
It was too loud to talk so everyone sang along.

THE RIGHT THING

As soon as the song was over, Justin, Jade, and Jordan jumped up and hurried to find Mom and Dad.

They told them about the wallet
and handed it to Mom.

Dad stood on tiptoes
and looked around.
Then he pointed.
"There's a lost-and-found booth,"
he said.
"They can help us find the owner."

On the way, Justin bumped
right into a clown!
They both jumped back.
The clown looked sad.
"Are you okay?" the clown
asked Justin.
"Yes," said Justin. "Are you?"

"No," said the sad clown.
"I lost my wallet."

Justin gasped. "What does it
look like?"
"It has red, yellow, and blue dots,"
said the clown,
"and pink and green stripes."

Justin smiled and said,
"My brother and sister and I
have something for you!"

"Dad! Mom! I found the owner
of the wallet!" Justin shouted.
Dad and Mom looked at Justin.
Jade and Jordan smiled.

Dad looked in the wallet.

He found a card with a photo.

The photo looked just like the clown.

Dad said, "Yes, you are right, Justin.

You have found the right owner."

Mom handed the wallet
to the clown.

"Thank you all so much!"
said the clown.
Then he pulled some money
out of the wallet
and said to Justin,
"Here is a reward for being honest."

Mom shook her head.
"No, thank you.
We're very proud of our kids
for doing the right thing.
That's all the reward they need."

"Well then, how about these?"
said the clown.
And like magic, three balloons
popped out of his sleeve!

"Wow!" Justin shouted.
"Clowns are really cool."
"Really?" Jordan and Jade laughed.
"Yes!" Justin said. "They are my
favorite part of a parade!"